MW01047526

The Adventures of Konrad the Kamel

Wanderlust
Book One

Written by Anna Dalhaimer Bartkowski
Illustrated by Elizabeth Koch

Anna Dalhaimer Bartkowski

Elizabeth Koch
8/2024

American Historical Society of Germans from Russia

The Adventures of Konrad the Kamel
Wanderlust

Published by American Historical Society of Germans from Russia.
Lincoln, Nebraska.

Bartkowski, Anna Dalhaimer - Writer
Koch, Elizabeth - Illustrator
The Adventures of Konrad the Kamel, Book One, Wanderlust
Book design by Anna Dalhaimer Bartkowski, Elizabeth Koch, and AHSGR

Printed in the United States of America
Library of Congress Control Number: 2024911566
ISBN Hard cover: 978-1-957061-10-8
ISBN Paperback: 978-1-957061-11-5

Camel Photographs used with permission courtesy of the AHSGR Archives and Dee Hert.

For the descendants of Germans from Russia and all who wander

and for the child still to be found in all of us.

Reviews of The Adventures of Konrad the Kamel

"Konrad the Kamel introduces the forgotten role that Bactrian Camels played when our German ancestors lived in the Russian Empire. This book provides an entertaining way to introduce new generations to their Germans from Russia heritage." - **Bob Ahlbrandt, AHSGR President**

"I love the book! My favorite line is 'wanderlust was in their genes.' I've always felt I have wanderlust in my blood!!"
- **Diane Bates, AHSGR Board Member**

"Cute Konrad — so helpful and brave. Kids will love him!" - **Karen Soeken, Past AHSGR President**

"The story of Konrad the Kamel is not only entertaining but extremely educational and very well written. If you have ever wondered why your German Russian ancestors used camels for field work, getting around and numerous other tasks, this story will answer your questions."
- **Dodie Rotherham, Past AHSGR President and host of Treffen Tuesday**

If you like this book, please leave a review on **Goodreads.com**
https://www.goodreads.com/book/show/214980796-the-adventures-of-konrad-the-kamel-wanderlust-book-one

Find out more information about Germans from Russia, at ahsgr.org.

Map of Russia, Mongolia and China, circa 1800s where Bactrian camels originated and lived

Not drawn to scale

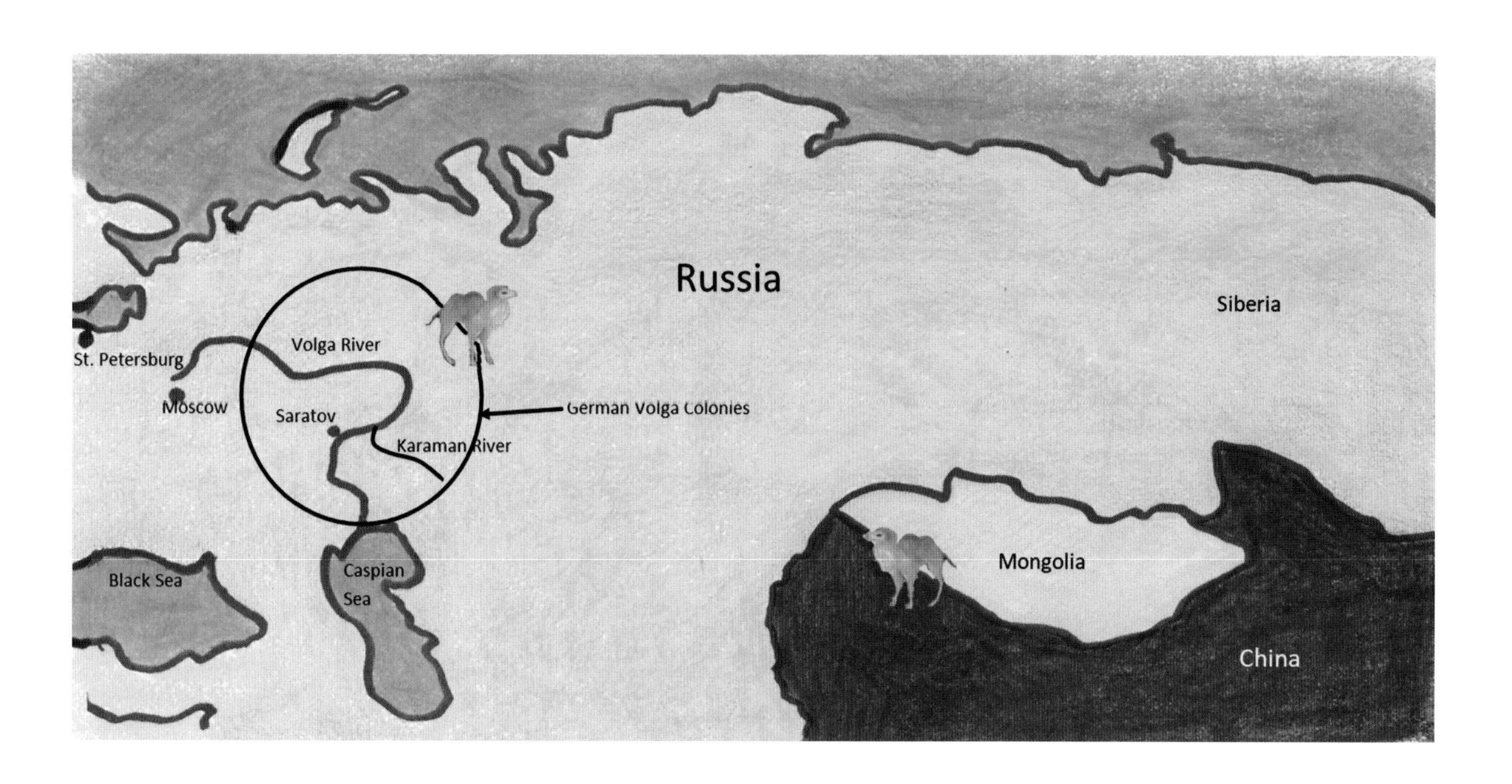

In a small Russian village settled by Germanic immigrants, young Konrad the Kamel lived with his family. Curious and adventurous, he often wandered off to explore the beautiful natural steppes surrounded by golden fields. It was still cold, and early spring buds sprouted despite the risk of another freeze.

His mother, Kara, favored Konrad because he reminded her of how she wandered when she was a child. Wanderlust was in their genes. She loved to spend her days with him while the rest of their family worked with the German farmers who came from western Europe to settle this land.

Konrad loved to sniff the grasses, nibbling a bit here and there. He loved to roam through clusters of trees, eating branches and dried leaves. He rambled to the Karaman River inhaling the damp air near the water. He strolled to the wild blueberry fields and munched stems since camels could eat bushes and dried grasses. Next he would visit the wildflower patch.

"Mother, I love our days together. Will we explore the countryside forever?"

"We'll explore like this for the next few months. Soon you will be old enough to help with the farmer's work. Together we will walk to the fields, pulling wagons, helping to carry seeds, planting spring crops, and bringing home the fall harvest." Kara lifted her head toward their home at the Bauer family homestead.

Back home, Konrad's older brother Kaleb greeted them. "I see you are back from your lazy, grazing day. We workers just returned, too. We worked hard all day. Oh, the burdens we carry and the challenges we face. Howling wolves chased us, but unlike you, we raced fast and escaped."

Kabir, their father, frowned at his oldest son. "Enough fibbing, Kaleb. We did not hear wolves today. You know you did not work until you were four years old. When Konrad is four, he will join our work." He settled next to Kara and nuzzled her neck.

While Kaleb strutted to show off, Konrad hung his head in embarrassment. He had heard stories from the wiser camels that the grey wolf was their only predator in this region. Tired of his brother's teasing, he left the courtyard and headed to the barns to get away from Kaleb.

Inside the barn, his grandfather, Kingston, lay near bundles of hay near the empty horse stalls. Konrad settled down next to him. “Grandpa, I love to roam and wander the fields. Work sounds hard. Do I have to work?”

Kingston breathed in deeply, his nostrils flaring. “All of us had to grow up and work at some point, Konrad. Kaleb teases you because he misses the carefree time he used to spend with your mother. Once you work with the family, you will be one of the best.”

Konrad’s stomach grumbled with worry. “But I’m scared. I‘m not as fast or strong as Kaleb.”

“Neither was Kaleb at your age.” Kingston gazed lovingly into Konrad’s eyes. “Do you know what the name Konrad means?”

Konrad shook his head. “No.”

“Your name means brave and bold. As you grow bigger and stronger, your bravery and boldness will be unlike any other camel in history.”

Konrad’s eyes lit up in excitement and he smiled as he imagined himself all grown up.

Kingston’s head and neck were upright and regal, the sovereign of the world he surveyed. “Konrad, I savor all our time together. I love to share these stories with you. Do you know why the Bauer family prefers camels over horses?”

Again, Konrad shook his head side to side.

Kingston smiled. “Our ancestors traveled to these Russian steppes from Mongolia’s vast Gobi Desert. Our Bactrian Kamel relatives now live across Asia from eastern Turkey and China to Siberia. We prove our bravery by surviving in harsh climates. We help colonists thrive because we require less care than horses. We do not need water daily. The earth supplies our food. We forage for everything we need.”

Konrad understood this story. He scavenged for food every day and only needed to drink water occasionally. The wisdom of Kingston’s words and his grandfather’s comfort warmed his heart.

Two months later the camels celebrated Konrad's fourth birthday. He loved the attention he received but feared the hard work ahead of him. He would greatly miss wandering through the steppes when he had to pull a wagon and work every day.

Then, a few weeks after his birthday, Konrad and the camels shed their winter coats. The Bauer family gathered the wool and stored it carefully in their barrels. Konrad remembered earlier years when the family used the wool to make clothing and rugs. He had listened to their words, and although they lived on the steppes, he was told their language was German and they had traveled far to this new land, just like the Kamel family.

After the wool was collected and stored, the family sprinted in and out of the house carrying scythes, baskets, barrels, plows, and seeds. From Pa Bauer to Ma Bauer, to the oldest son Marcus, to the daughter Maria, and to the youngest son Anton they were busy organizing all the tools they needed. They pulled the wagon to the center of the courtyard. They loaded the saddlebags and tools in the wagon bed. It was the first time Anton helped with the work.

Konrad recognized the tools. Spring planting was expected any day. He gazed as the spring buds came to life, the petals venturing open toward the sun and basking in the warmer weather.

Konrad shuddered and shook his body and spit into the air. Turning four years old had come too soon for him.

When all the items were loaded onto the wagon, Kara nudged Konrad. “Now is the time for you and me to support our family. We will pull the wagon together leading everyone to the fields for planting.”

The sun shone brightly, and the world was painted in spring pastels. The day Konrad feared had arrived. He was hitched to the wagon next to his mother. It was not as uncomfortable as he anticipated and he liked being near his mother. Kingston, who stayed in the barn, nodded his approval to Konrad who smiled back at him.

Anton sat on the wagon with Pa Bauer, Ma Bauer, and Maria. Kaleb and Kabir were strong enough to carry loads in saddlebags directly on their backs. They walked through the gate and waited outside while Marcus locked the gate and jumped onto the wagon.

The group journeyed north to the family field. When they arrived, Pa Bauer unhitched Kara and Konrad. Kara nudged Konrad's back. "Do not stray far, we may be needed soon." Konrad smiled broadly, surprised they were free to roam. He walked to the grasses opposite the planting fields.

He sniffed the grasses, nibbling a bit here and there. He roamed through a cluster of trees eating a few dried leaves. He plodded to the edge of the Karaman River watching the water flow. He grazed in the wild blueberry patch and munched stems. He was grateful camels could chew thorny and hard vegetation. There was plenty of food here. Once Konrad finished foraging, he turned down to the wildflower path.

Something rustled in the bushes behind him. He turned to see Anton standing alone. Konrad walked to him and gently nudged his back with his nose. He pointed Anton to the fields where his parents were.

“Thank you. Yes, I understand, let’s go back.” Anton nodded and they walked together side by side back to their families.

Tired from his walk and his early morning chores, Anton climbed into the empty wagon, covered himself with a blanket, and laid his head down to rest.

Kara saw Konrad return and motioned to him to join her. She carried a small saddlebag full of seeds.

Pa Bauer lifted the other saddlebag onto Konrad who suddenly felt a surge of unknown strength through his body. He followed his mother to the far end of the field where Marcus waited for the seed they carried.

When the sun was directly overhead, the Bauer family stopped work and ate their noonday meal. The Kamels moved to the grassy area and ate off the land. After the break, Konrad noticed the family was distracted by dark clouds rolling quickly toward the fields on the southeast horizon.

The Bauers hurried to gather all their belongings back on the cart, lifting loads onto Kabir and Kaleb, and hitching Konrad and Kara to the wagon again.

The family jumped on the wagon where Anton slept covered with the blanket. With a flick of the reins, the Kamels galloped into the wind, heading home as fast as they could. As they raced, Konrad heard eerie wolves' howls in the distance.

Rain pelted the camels skin, which was no longer protected by their ample fur. The water bounced off the wagon. Lightning flashed and lit up the entire sky. Thunder rumbled so loudly Konrad's teeth rattled and he wished he could cover his ears.

Once in the home courtyard, the downpour pounded against the buildings. The Bauers pulled the wagon into the barn, got the saddlebags off Kabir and Kaleb, and unhitched Konrad and Kara. Kingston awoke from his afternoon nap surprised by the family's early return.

After unloading and drying their tools, the Bauers checked the wagon bed one last time. Ma Bauer lifted the blanket and gasped. “Where is Anton? I thought he was asleep in the wagon but he is not here.” Everyone searched around the wagon and in the courtyard.

Forked lightning sped across the sky. The loud clap of thunder shook Konrad to his bones. Pa Bauer’s forehead wrinkled in deep furrows as he frowned and forced back tears. “We must go to the house and light a fire so we can get dry. The storm is too dangerous for us to search for him.” Ma Bauer cried but nodded in agreement. Pa Bauer held the barn door open as the family members darted through the downpour toward their house, closing the barn door behind him.

Filled with guilt, Konrad swallowed hard, his eyes brimming with tears. “We must go find him! Anton followed me as I wandered on my little adventure and now he is lost and all on his own. It’s my fault.”

Kabir shuddered to shake the wet off his skin. “No, the weather is too dangerous. You saw the grasses bent flat with the wind, the earth sizzling where lightning scorched the ground. We are fortunate we arrived home. We will pray Anton finds shelter and will search for him once the storm passes. We must stay safe together.”

The young camel could not believe his father’s decision. He turned to look at his grandfather who said, “You must stay here, Konrad. We will search for Anton as soon as we can.”

Konrad pictured Anton alone and frightened in the storm. He prayed the wolves he heard journeyed in the opposite direction. *It was my fault the boy had wandered from the fields. All because I wanted an adventure.*

Later that night, when the others fell asleep, Konrad left the barn and hazarded his first steps back into the storm leaving the gate slightly ajar behind him.

Dust and rain swirled, and thunder crashed around him. Konrad closed his slit nostrils to protect him from breathing in the dirt and water flying through the air. He used his keen eyes to navigate through the chaos.

He galloped fast to the planting field. He ran the length and depth of the area, bleating and bellowing with all his might, hoping Anton would hear him. He circled the area twice.

No Anton.

He raced through grasses back and forth and forth and back not stopping to nibble a bite. He grunted and hoped Anton would hear him. He bounded through the grasses checking the high spots and the low crevices.

Where was Anton?

Konrad dashed to the cluster of trees. Looking up to the treetops and below to the roots, he checked if Anton sought shelter in tree branches or trunks.

Where was Anton?

Konrad sped to the shore of the Karaman River. He looked left and right, then right and left.

Where was Anton?

He sprinted to the wild blueberry fields, yet he did not stop to eat. He simply ran up and down, then down and up the rows of plants.

Still, no Anton.

He flew to the wildflower patch, the thunder growing louder and louder with every step. The rain slowed its pounding and the lightning brightened his view. In the far corner of the path close to the woods he saw a completely still figure. Konrad approached it slowly holding his breath. *Could it be Anton? Please let him be alive!*

Konrad bent his nose to the ground and nudged Anton. The boy stirred, then awoke with a jolt as the thunder cracked and the lightning struck against the sky.

Anton cried out in fear. Tears puddled in his eyes until he recognized his camel friend. Konrad was so happy to find him that he sank to his knees and flicked his head so Anton would climb on his back. Anton mounted the camel, and when Konrad was certain Anton had grabbed onto his remaining fur, he stood up. Once Anton was secure and safe on his back, he gently edged his way toward the village. They still had to cross the dangerous, open fields in the dead of night.

After a few minutes of strolling gently, he hurried his steps to reach home as quickly as possible. When they were less than halfway home, Konrad heard the growl of a grey wolf. He looked to his right and saw the leader of the pack ready to pounce. No time to waste. Konrad pushed every muscle he had to the limit and zipped out of the area. All the wolves chased, united in their hunger. As Konrad ran for a few miles with the wolves in quick pursuit, he counted at least five wolves. He and Anton were severely outnumbered.

Konrad heard the wolves panting and getting closer and closer. He felt the hot breath of the lead wolf near his legs. Konrad's legs were his strength so he quickly kicked out his back legs and directly hit the leader who yelped in pain and fell to the ground.

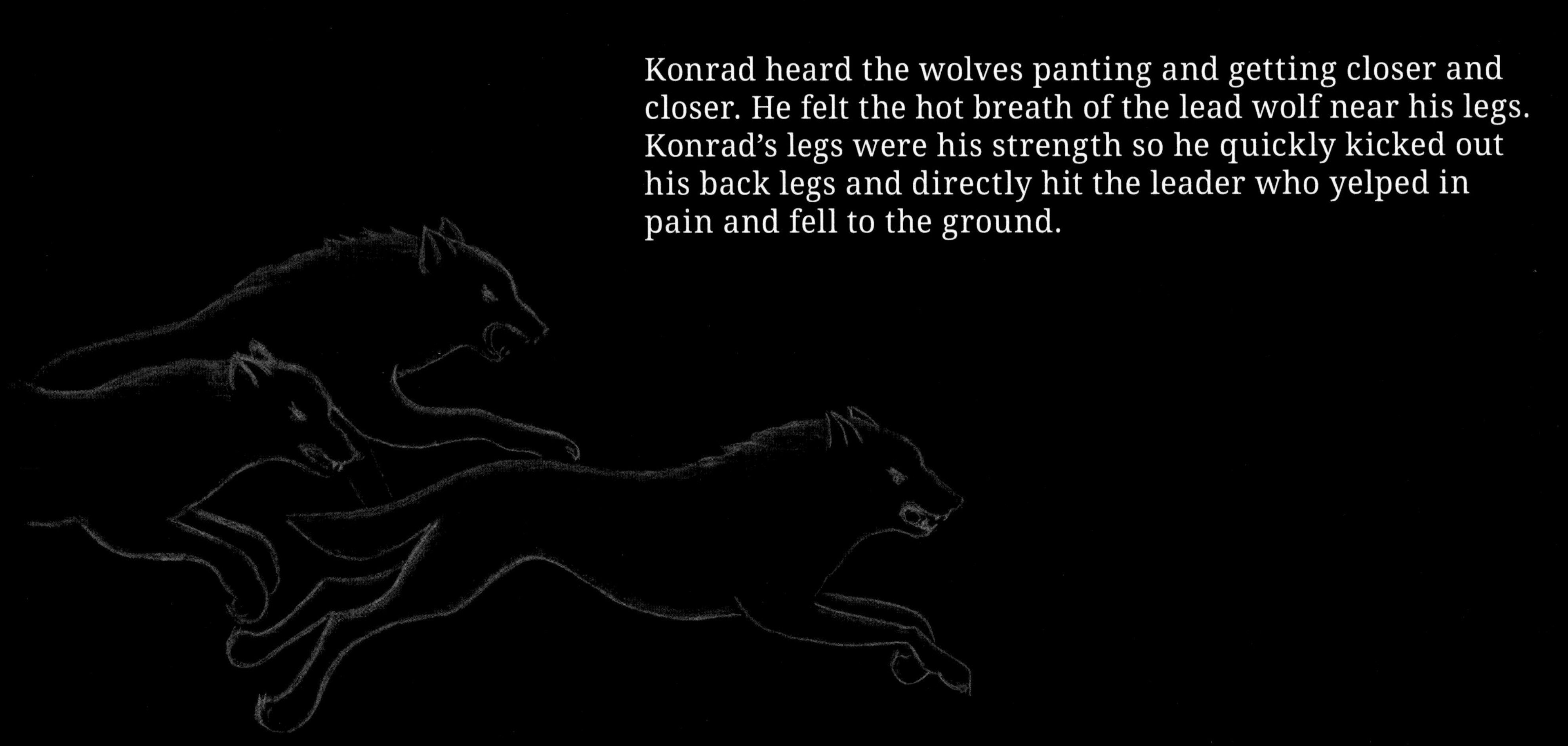

The other wolves ignored the fallen, but it ignited their fury and fueled their hunger, so they leapt into a faster pace. Invigorated by adrenaline, Konrad kicked the next wolf on his side and sped up faster than he had ever run.

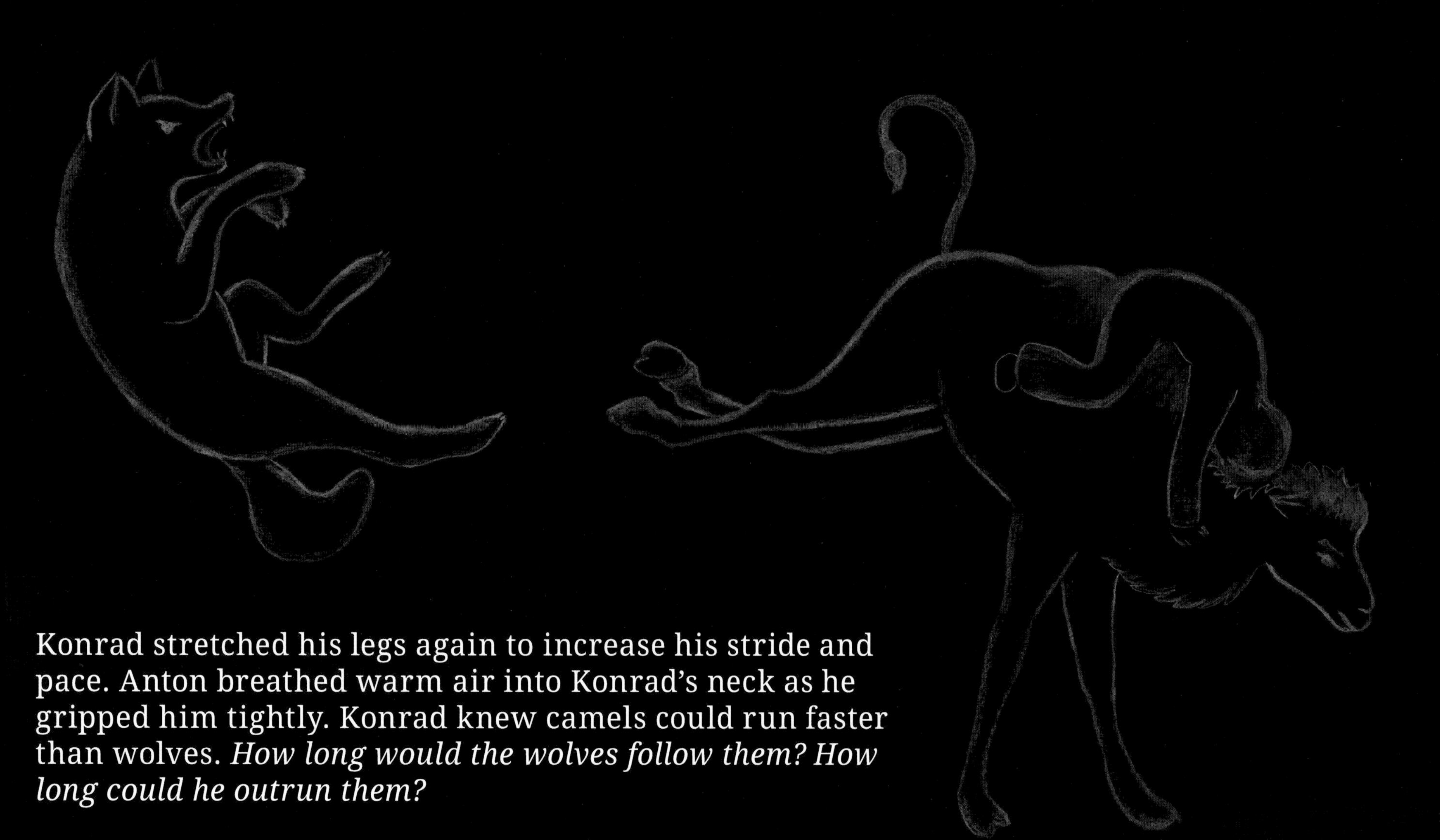

Konrad stretched his legs again to increase his stride and pace. Anton breathed warm air into Konrad's neck as he gripped him tightly. Konrad knew camels could run faster than wolves. *How long would the wolves follow them? How long could he outrun them?*

Lightning illuminated the village in the distance. He plotted his course to where he left the barnyard gate slightly open. Konrad ran and ran and ran. When he arrived in the village, he flew to the gate's entrance and slid to a stop. He banged the ajar gate open and jumped into the courtyard. Glancing back, he saw the wolves, and slammed the gate shut on them.

He heard mournful growling as the wolves pounded ferociously against the gate. After a few minutes, their loud howls echoed as they left the village.

The rain slowed to a drizzle. As the storm dissipated, the clouds broke open revealing slivers of the rising sun shining through the dark clouds. Konrad stood silently, catching his breath after his incredible run.

Kaleb heard the gate slam and was the first one out of the barn. "Baby brother, you look like you ran the race of your life."

Konrad knelt down, allowing Anton to slip off to the ground. He hugged Konrad around his neck, not wanting to leave him.

Kingston stood the tallest, beaming with pride at his grandson. “Konrad, you risked your life to save this boy. You are brave and bold. You have earned the name Konrad today.”

Kabir and Kara nuzzled their noses onto Konrad’s back.

Awakened by the howling wolves, the Bauers ran out of their house. Ma and Pa Bauer cried out "Anton" when they saw their youngest son, and embraced him in a big hug while he raved about how the camel had saved him. Marcus and Maria looked in awe at Konrad. The Bauers beamed with joy and bowed their heads murmuring thanks to him. Then they looked back at Anton. "Let's get you out of these wet clothes."

Konrad shook himself, spraying water on everyone. The Bauers rejoiced in laughter and the Kamels stood proudly next to Konrad. Anton turned to Konrad. “The sun will dry us soon. And we will be best friends for the rest of our lives.”

Surrounded by his family, Konrad’s bravery and boldness became a legend told time and time again in the heart of the small village.

A note from the Author

When my grandmother told me she grew up around camels in Russia, I was curious and intrigued. Years later I saw pictures of the camels helping the German Russian settlers, but it wasn't just any kind of camel, it was a Bactrian camel, native to China and Mongolia. Their most distinguishing feature is that they have two humps. Dromedary camels, or Arabians, have one hump. Camels are unique creatures and here are some of the questions and answers I learned about them.

What are the camels' humps?

Both Bactrian and dromedary camels store fat, not water, in their humps. They use the fat to survive when food and water are scarce.

Why are the words camel and Kamel used in this book?

Camel is an English word while Kamel is the German word to describe a Bactrian or dromedary. For this book, Kamel is the last name of the camel family, hence Konrad the Kamel.

Why did German Russia Settlers use camels?

Camels are born with unique features making them ideal to help the Germans in Russia. Camels can travel for miles and miles without water or food. Horses, on the other hand, require water, grains, oats, or hay every day. Camels were easier to care for since they forage for food, eating brittle brush and leaves, then slowly digesting food through their three stomachs. They also have multiple rows of long eyelashes to ward off dust and they can close their nostrils so they don't inhale sand or dirt from storms or their environment.

When did camels arrive in Russia?

Prior to the Germans settling in Russia, many tribes and nomads used these lands as caravan trade routes and grazing pasture for their animals. Camels as pack animals carried goods for travelers and merchants. The Ottoman Empire was well known for trading camels at markets. Bactrians have been on the steppes and Black Sea regions as people traversed across the steppes for centuries. Borders changed frequently here.

The AHSGR News E-blast of January 2023 shared that in the centuries long Russo-Turkish Wars, Russia won partitions of land from the Ottoman Empire in 1791. Later wars including the Russo-Armenian and the Russo-Japanese wars created much travel though these areas.

While it's uncertain who was the first German Russian settler to use camels, there are references to camels in numerous sources.

- *The Story of Johann* by Mela Meisner Lindsay is about a young lad from Kratzke who longed to Come to Amerika. Lindsay wrote about camels when she describes the daily village chores. She wrote, "But what gave Johann the biggest thrill of all was to see tall and lanky Alek jolting astride a winter-shaggy camel with ten more equally shaggy creatures following behind."
- In an extract from *The Sword and Pen*, author Rudolf Stratz wrote about his grandfather Sebastian Stratz. "When he died at the age of 70, he owned a whole street full of houses, where, in my youth, camels still walked and the wild yellow hounds of a Turkish city tramped around."
- In *The Letters from Hell 1922*, on May 15 it was written: "Things are easier now, everything looks good for this year and there should be a good harvest, but now there is a shortage of working livestock. I have one Camel and now I have to buy another but it is so outrageously expensive—from 200 Million per head."
- In *Wir Wollen Deutsche Bleiben*, we see a picture of a camel pulling a wagon with the caption, "Volga Germans made good use of the Bactrian camel, one of the hallmarks of their routines that did not make the transition to the U.S."

Did you find other references to camels? If so, please share with me at anna@bart4.com.

Sources

AHSGR E-blast email, January 23, 2023.

Lindsay, Mela Meisner. *The Story of Johann, The Boy Who Longed to Come to Amerika.* American Historical Society of Germans from Russia. Lincoln, Nebraska. 1988. Pg 4.

Retrieved from https://www.blackseagr.org/pdfs/konrad/Extract%20from%20Sword%20and%20Pen.pdf on May 16, 2024.

Walters, George J. *Wir Wollen Deutsche Bleiben,* American Historical Society of Germans from Russia. Lincoln, Nebraska. 2021. Pg. xxxi.

About the Author

Anna Dalhaimer Bartkowski's journey from building snow forts in Sheboygan, Wisconsin, to uncovering her German Russian heritage is as thrilling as a touchdown at Lambeau Field! As a kid, she traded snowball fights for softball tournaments and swapped hot cocoa for brat fries, all while pledging lifelong loyalty to the Green Bay Packers.

But Anna's curiosity went beyond her backyard adventures. At a young age, she wondered about her missing grandparents and the mysterious German-speaking ancestors who lived in Russia. This sparked her lifelong quest to unearth her family's history, sending her on genealogical escapades.

After earning a bachelor's degree in journalism and marketing from Marquette University (and witnessing some epic Al McGuire NCAA basketball moments), Anna dove headfirst into the world of newspaper advertising. But her career path took a turn when she landed in Arizona, reigniting her passion for her roots.

Joining the Arizona Sun Chapter and becoming a life member of AHSGR fueled Anna's quest even more. She traced her lineage back to the original settlers of Mariental, Reinwald, Balzer, and Rosenfeld am Nachoi uncovering a rich tapestry of heritage spanning villages in modern day Germany and Luxembourg.

Anna didn't stop at uncovering her family's past. She brought their stories to life through captivating books like *Dead Reckoning: A Rosalind Schmidt Genealogical Mystery* and *Value Meals on the Volga*. Her dedication to preserving German Russian culture led her to edit collections like *Thirty Years in the Desert* and contribute to anthologies on authorship.

Not content with just writing about history, Anna became an avid member of AHSGR, serving in various leadership roles and spearheading initiatives to connect members worldwide. Travel was imminent, from AHSGR conventions to Argentina. Perhaps the most thrilling discovery was finding descendants of cousins who survived exile in Siberia, bridging gaps across continents and generations, including a poignant journey to Germany where she bonded with long-lost cousins.

But with every adventure, Anna's enthusiasm for storytelling and family history only grows, inviting others to join her on the journey at annabartkowski.com.

From snowball fights to family reunions, Anna's tale is a whirlwind of discovery, proving that the past is never truly buried—it's waiting to be explored with boundless curiosity and a sprinkle of Sheboygan magic!

About the Illustrator

Elizabeth Koch is a self-taught artist who grew up in a small town in northwest Kansas, living near her German Russian Grandmother Basgall-Koch who taught her how to crochet, make rag rugs and make home-made noodles (dried over the back of a chair, of course) for Grandma's tasty chicken noodle soup, which always appeared when anyone in the family was ill.

Her grandmother was born in Pfeiffer, Rush, Kansas, one of the early German Russian settlements in Kansas, but never spoke of her background. Her son thought it was because she, and many of the German Russians, in their early years in America, were often ridiculed for their Russian-like clothing and called Russkies, though they identified only as Germans.

Elizabeth's original German-Russian ancestor Jean Pasqual had a French not a German surname, was a hatmaker by trade, not a farmer, and originally settled in the Volga French settlement of Franzosen on 26 Aug 1766, moving his family a year later to the German settlement of Rothammel where "Pasqual" became "Basgal" and later Basgall.

In 1876 her Grandmother Koch's parents [Joseph K Basgall (Rothammel colony) and Katharina Falkenstein (Schuck colony)]—and almost the entire Basgall family—moved to either Ellis or Rush Counties, Kansas.

Education was important to the German Russians, and to her Grandmother, who passed on a love of learning to her children and who then passed it on to Elizabeth's generation.

Elizabeth's education includes a BA in history and chemistry from Kansas State University; German language studies as an exchange student at Justus Liebig University in Giessen, Germany; 3 years history studies and Master's thesis research on a Fulbright-Swiss Universities' Government Grant at the University of Bern, Switzerland, leading to her Master's degree in Renaissance and Reformation history from Kansas State, where she was also a graduate teaching assistant.

She obtained her Medical Degree from Kansas University in Kansas City, did her residency in Radiology at Baylor College of Medicine in Houston, Texas, spent years in private practice, and later joined the Radiology Teaching Faculty at Baylor in Houston.

Upon retirement, she and her husband returned to his Cajun roots in Louisiana. She is on the board of the American Historical Society of Germans from Russia (AHSGR), enjoys making picture quilts for family and for fund raisers for animal rescue groups. Due to a Luxembourg ancestor, she also is also among the volunteers at Luxroots.org, whose goal it is to input information from all available Luxembourgish documents (birth, marriage, death, censuses, etc.) in a data base for present and future generations of historians and family researchers. During Covid she used her art to illustrate greeting cards for a retirement community.

The first book she illustrated was Anne Stang's *Anna's Red Purse*, available through AHSGR at https://ahsgr.org/product/annas-red-purse/.